I0748488

CorpSpace

Books by David Dvorkin

Fiction

The Arm and Flanagan

Budspy

Business Secrets from the Stars

Cage of Bone

The Cavaradossi Killings

Central Heat

The Children of Shiny Mountain

Children of the Undead

CorpSpace

Damon the Caiman

Dawn Crescent (with Daniel Dvorkin)

Earthmen and Other Aliens

The Green God

Pit Planet

The Prisoner of the Blood series

Insatiable

Unquenchable

Randolph Runner

The Seekers

Slit

Time and the Soldier

Time for Sherlock Holmes

Ursus

Star Trek

The Trellisane Confrontation
Time Trap
The Captains' Honor (with Daniel Dvorkin)

Nonfiction

At Home with Solar Energy
The Dead Hand of Mrs. Stifle
Dust Net
Once a Jew, Always a Jew?
Self–Publishing Tools, Tips, and Techniques
The Surprising Benefits of Being Unemployed
When We Landed on the Moon: A Memoir

CorpSpace

A Flight of Fancy

David Dvorkin

Editing, print layout, e–book conversion,
and cover design by DLD Books

DLD Books
www.dldbooks.com
Editing and Self–Publishing Services

ISBN: 978-1-7362886-7-2

Contents

Introduction

If you've worked in a corporation, you have probably felt sometimes that the corporation had a personality of its own, something more than the sum of the personalities of the people working there. The corporation had the feel of a living entity—and not a friendly one.

A small company, especially a startup, can feel friendly and relaxed. However, that changes when the company grows past a certain size. In my experience, that's somewhere between 50 and 100 employees. From that point on, the corporation's personality is colder, more distant, blunter, harder, tougher, impersonal. Those traits intensify as the corporation continues to grow.

Of course, that impression is entirely subjective. Corporations aren't living entities, and they don't have personalities. They are soulless, brainless organizations, and if they behave badly, then the blame for that falls on the shoulders of the people in charge, the men and women in the C–Suite, as it's sometimes called, the top floor of the corporation's high–rise headquarters, where the offices are huge and so are the salaries and perks, where dwell the lords and ladies with titles beginning with the letter C: CEO, CTO, CIO, COO, etc.

But what if there is something to the feeling that the corporation you work for has a personality? What if the corporation is, in some sense, a living being?

But in what sense?

Certainly not in the same sense as a human or a dog or a cat. (If only corporations were as loyal to their employees as dogs are to their humans!) After all, you can look up the records detailing the origin and history of a corporation, from its foundation to the present. People created the organization out of nothing and have shepherded it ever since. Their names are on record.

Or so it seems.

What if it is not as it seems? Perhaps many, even most, of the entities that we perceive as corporations are in actuality just the visible parts of living beings that exist in higher-dimensional space.

Here begins the flight of fancy.

Flatland and More

But first, bear with me while I lay some groundwork. This will be just a brief digression, and then we'll return to the fun stuff.

As we all know, we live in a three-dimensional universe, the three dimensions being length, width, and height. Everything we experience in our daily lives, including us, has length, width, and height.

Now try to imagine that instead of living in our familiar three-dimensional world, you're living in a two-dimensional one. The world is as flat as a table top. Everything, including you, has width and length but not height. Everything is utterly flat. There are no mountains or valleys anywhere. You can move forwards and backwards and from side to side, but you can never move up and down. In fact, there is no such thing as up or down! You don't even know that up and down exist. If someone from our three-dimensional world tried to describe up and down to you, you'd think he was a babbling idiot.

Back in 1884, using the pseudonym A. Square, an English schoolteacher named Edwin Abbott Abbott (that's not a typo) published a delightful short novel about such a world. The title of the novel is *Flatland: A Romance of Many Dimensions.* It describes a world in which there is no up or down. Everything exists on a plane, just like the one you probably remember from high school geometry. There are living, intelligent beings in Flatland. Like us, they have houses, families, jobs, and so on, but unlike us, they have no knowledge of up or down. They have no height, no third dimension. They are completely flat. They have no thickness.

(Actually, in the book, the Flatlanders do have a microscopic bit of thickness, of height. I don't think Abbott should have written it that way, so I'll pretend he didn't.)

In Abbott's novel, the beings who live in Flatland are the geometrical shapes you remember from those geometry classes—squares, triangles, circles, etc. One Flatlander, a square, is visited by a sphere from outside Flatland, that is to say, from the three-dimensional universe.

(In the novel, the three-dimensional beings are also geometrical shapes, but they are three-dimensional ones, such as spheres, instead of people like us. I'm sure Abbott had a reason for not making them normal humans, although I can't imagine what it was.)

The sphere struggles to explain three dimensions to the square. The square refuses to believe him, insisting that nothing exists outside Flatland, and the idea of a third dimension is absurd. The sphere gives up arguing, yanks the square off the flat surface of Flatland, and shows him the bigger universe in which Flatland floats.

This is quite an experience for the square. His mind racing, he wonders if there are even higher dimensions. Just as Flatland exists inside a three-dimensional universe, he speculates, might not the three-dimensional universe exist inside a four-dimensional one? And the four-dimensional one inside a five-dimensional one? And so on, endlessly upward and outward into higher and higher dimensions. The sphere is angered by this speculation. He is as unable to conceive of such higher-dimensional universes as the square was at first unable to conceive of a three-dimensional world.

When the sphere first tells the square about up and down, the words mean nothing to the square, for he has never experienced anything but forwards and backwards and left and right, and the same is true for everyone else in Flatland.

You and I are much like the square, the Flatlander. We can move in three dimensions—side to side, forwards and backwards, and up and down—but that's all. Try to imagine moving in a fourth direction, a direction that is at right angles to side to side, forwards and backwards, and up and down. We don't even know what it is we're trying to imagine. We can describe that idea mathematically, but we can't directly experience it.

What if there is such a direction, even though we can't experience it? What if a universe of more than three dimensions exists, and our three-dimensional universe is contained inside it? What would that higher-dimensional universe be like? Do living beings exist there? What are they like?

I'm going to tell you about that universe, the beings who live there, and how they affect our universe. First, though, let's talk about intersections and projections.

Intersections

Look at the illustration below. It shows a sphere hovering about a flat surface. Imagine that this is the sphere that visited

Flatland, and imagine also that the flat surface below it is Flatland. The sphere is on its way down to begin the visit.

Suppose you are one of the inhabitants of Flatland. Maybe you're even the square featured in Abbott's novel. As long as the sphere is hovering above Flatland, you are completely unaware of its existence because you can't look up to see it. You have no concept of "up."

But now the sphere moves down until it is just touching Flatland.

You can now see the part of it that's touching Flatland. It's just a point. You are confused. Why did this point suddenly appear out of nowhere?

Now the sphere moves down still further, so that a small part of is below Flatland, while most of is still above. What can you, the Flatlander, see of the sphere now? Just a circle, a slice through the sphere.

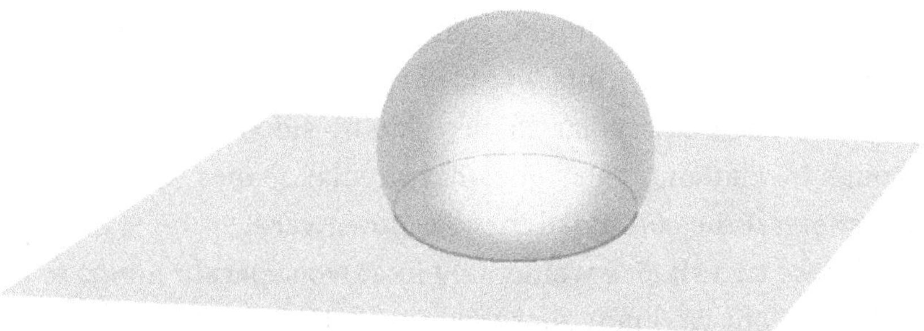

If the sphere continues to move downward, the circle will grow. Once the middle of the sphere has passed through Flatland, the circle will start shrinking. Eventually, it will be only a point again, and then even that will disappear.

You can see why this is so confusing to the Flatlander. How can he possibly understand what he's seeing? Perhaps if he were mathematically gifted, he could figure it out, but it would be quite a mental stretch for him.

What's happening is obvious to us only because we have the advantage of seeing the whole picture instead of just the small part that the Flatlander sees. The Flatlander can only see the part of the sphere that intersects his universe. That part, the circle that seems to grow and shrink for no reason, is called the intersection of the sphere and the plane.

We use the word "intersection" in that sense in our normal, daily lives without thinking twice about it. For instance, we call the place where two streets meet an intersection. "Intersect" is also a verb. We talk about two paths intersecting.

The sphere and Flatland make for a very simple intersection. What if the object intersecting Flatland is more complicated than the sphere? What would the intersection look like then?

That would depend on the object.

For example, suppose a naked man moved down through Flatland. First, two footprints would appear in Flatland as the soles of the man's feet intersected Flatland. As he continued to move down, the footprints would shrink and would be replaced by two somewhat circular shapes side by side—his legs, sliced through by Flatland. The somewhat circular shapes would grow in diameter as he continued to move downward.

These two shapes would look like two separate things to a Flatlander, but we know that they aren't, that they're all part of the same three–dimensional object.

As he continued to move down through Flatland, the two slices through his legs would merge into one, a slice through his body. The Flatlander would see the two roughly circular shapes suddenly merge into a much larger, somewhat circular shape.

Then his fingertips would intersect Flatland—four small circles on each side of the body–circle. Those would be joined by two more small circles, his thumbs, one on each side of his body next to the four finger–circles on each side. After a short time, all of those would merge into the two circles caused by his arms.

Then everything would merge into a much smaller circle, his neck. That circle would expand a bit as his head moved down through Flatland. There would be a bulge in front caused by his nose and two more bulges, one on each side, caused by his ears. Eventually, only the very top of the man's head would appear in Flatland. That would diminish to a point, which would finally disappear as he moved all the way below Flatland, no longer in contact with it at all.

How strange and disorienting this would be to our Flatlander! Even if he were the mathematically gifted being I mentioned above, it's unlikely that he would be able to deduce what was happening and what kind of being was causing these phenomena.

Is that not complicated enough for you? Then imagine an octopus intersecting with Flatland instead of a man, or a jellyfish instead of a man, or a millipede. Our poor Flatlander might think he was going mad.

Now let's really stretch our imaginations.

Suppose that Flatland just happens to slice through—intersect—a giant corporation here in our three-dimensional world. Yes, a whole corporation!

We need a name for this hypothetical corporation. Let's call it Glittering Euphemisms, or GE for short. Think of Flatland as a super-thin and extremely large and very flat sheet of paper. Now imagine this sheet of paper slicing through many of the buildings, desks, chairs, people, delivery trucks, and so on in GE locations all across the world.

(But imagine that this slicing does no damage. It doesn't result in blood and guts all over the place. Let's not complicate our story.)

The Flatlander would see these many intersections as two-dimensional buildings, desks, chairs, etc., all of which they have in Flatland. Perhaps he would even recognize that they were all connected. He might see all of them in combination as a Flatland corporation. He might even apply for a job at Flatland GE, completely unaware that what he thinks is a corporation is actually just the intersection of his two-dimensional universe with a three-dimensional corporation.

Now imagine that the people in the real GE, the three-dimensional one, are aware of what's going on. They can look down into Flatland and see this intersection situation, and it amuses them to toy with the Flatlander. So the intersection of a GE Human Resources employee, who appears to the Flatlander to be a two-dimensional HR person, interviews him, and he ends up being hired.

The poor flat fellow could spend his entire career working for Flatland GE, eventually retiring on his meager pension, without ever realizing that everything he thought was real was an illusion.

Or was it an illusion? We'll return to this later.

Projections

Let's go back to the sphere in the novel *Flatland*. Imagine that the country where the sphere lives in three-dimensional space is a harsh dictatorship and that the sphere, having broken one of his country's many laws, has just been condemned to a period of exile in Flatland. A giant machine is used to violently squash him flatter than any pancake, so flat that he is indistinguishable from the circles who live in Flatland. He is then dumped in Flatland, where he will have to stay for the duration of his sentence.

(Of course, for this to work, we have to imagine that he's able to survive this squashing instead of being converted to a horrifying mess of blood and guts. Let's suppose that that's not a problem.)

Imagine the torture of his punishment! Not only is he cut

off from contact with everyone he loves, just like prisoners in our own world, but in addition, he can't even see his world. He's now a Flatlander. He can't look up or down. If he tries to talk to his now–fellow Flatlanders about the three–dimensional universe he came from, they will think him a lunatic and will lock him up in one of their two–dimensional insane asylums.

This conversion of a three–dimensional sphere to a two–dimensional circle is an example of a projection.

(The mathematical definition of "projection" is more abstract and complex than this example and of course includes nothing about nauseating splatters of blood and guts. Perhaps mathematics would be of greater interest to more people if it did.)

A sphere is a simple shape, and its two–dimensional projection, a circle, is also simple. As is the case with intersections, the projection will be more complicated if the three–dimensional object being projected into Flatland is more complicated than a sphere. If the object is a human being, for example, then the two–dimensional projection will depend on the orientation of the human being squashed, the position of his arms and legs at squashing time, and various other factors.

Squashing is one way of projecting three–dimensional objects down onto Flatland. Another way is shadows.

We're all familiar with the parlor game where someone holds his hands in front of a bright light in such a way that a shadow that looks like, say, a rabbit is projected onto a wall.

Let's suppose that the bright sun of the three–dimensional world suddenly starts shining down onto Flatland. The coming and going of the light is very mysterious to Flatlanders, but even more mysterious are the shadows of three–dimensional objects cast down onto Flatland by the sun. Remember that Flatlanders have never seen shadows. Being only two–dimensional objects, they don't cast shadows. Suddenly, strange dark shapes—the two-dimensional shadows of three-dimensional objects or people—appear out of nowhere, move around unpredictably, and then vanish.

Simple 3D objects like spheres cast simple shadows—circles, in the case of spheres. You've probably seen photographs taken from space showing the circular shadow of the moon moving across the Earth during a solar eclipse. It's the same phenomenon.

If the object casting the shadow is more complex, such as a man, then so is the shadow. As the man moves through the sunlight and moves his arms and legs about, his shadow on Flatland moves and changes shape. It might bear little relationship to the man himself.

That's strange enough. Now imagine that the three-dimensional object casting the shadow is an octopus or a millipede. And it's moving all of its tentacles or legs. How creepy those shadows would be!

What do Flatlanders make of this? How do they explain the shadows? Perhaps they have evolved a complex belief system about ghosts and a spirit world. Or perhaps they have created a complex theology about some kind of heaven and divine beings.

(Theology is the same thing as believing in ghosts, of course.)

Suppose the object blocking the three-dimensional sun is huge, enough to cast a completely black shadow over a vast stretch of inhabited Flatland. How terrifying that would be to the Flatlanders! They would shiver in fear in that awful darkness for a period of time that would seem to them interminable until the shadow moved away and light returned.

The moon's shadow sweeps over the surface of the Earth repeatedly. That's caused by the moon moving between us and the sun. It's what we call a solar eclipse. Ancient people recorded those eclipses and learned that there was a pattern to eclipses. They learned to predict eclipses, even though they didn't understand what caused the pattern. In time, we figured out that the moon orbits the Earth and the Earth orbits the sun, and the combination of those motions explains solar eclipses, lunar eclipses (the Earth casting its shadow on the moon), and the phases of the moon.

In the case of Flatland, if the obscuring object is orbiting the three-dimensional sun in such a way that that its shadow sweeps over Flatland in repeating patterns, perhaps some brilliant Flatlander will deduce what's happening in three-dimensional space to cause that pattern. But his intellectual task will be far more difficult than it was for our scientists to figure out how lunar and solar eclipses work. Our scientists live in three-dimensional space, the same three-dimensional space as the sun, moon, and Earth, and we can all observe the sun and moon and watch the moon rise and set. Even so, it took an immense span of time for human beings to work out how the sun, the moon, and the Earth—and the planets, for that matter—all move in relation to each other. Imagine the brainpower required of that Flatlander genius to duplicate that intellectual achievement and to understand that those planetary movements are happening in three dimensions.

Try to imagine strange shadows appearing on the ground in front of you, growing and shrinking, twisting, changing shape, disappearing without any light or obscuring object that you can see to explain the phenomenon. Then someone says to you, "Oh, those are actually three-dimensional shadows being cast onto our world by a four-dimensional creature moving around in the light of a four-dimensional sun."

"What?" you reply. "You're crazy. Where are this sun and

this creature?"

"I told you. They're outside our three–dimensional universe, out in four–dimensional space."

"Where? Point to them!"

"Well, that's just it. I can't, because it's impossible to point in that fourth direction, just as it's impossible for a Flatlander to point up."

"You're crazy."

As Below, So Above

A sphere is the three-dimensional version of a circle. In the world of mathematics, this trend continues into higher dimensions. For example, a hypersphere is the four-dimensional version of a sphere.

What does a hypersphere look like? I have no idea. I'm trapped in three dimensions with you, and I can't look out into the four-dimensional world that surrounds our three-dimensional one. All of these concepts exist in mathematics and can be described using the language of mathematics, but we can't actually experience them directly. We don't even know if they exist in reality or if they're just mathematical concepts.

Let's suppose they do exist. When the sphere intersected Flatland, it looked like a circle to the Flatlander. If a hypersphere intersected our three-dimensional world, it would look to us like a sphere.

With four dimensions available, however, there could be all kinds of weird shapes out there in that universe surrounding ours. What would they look like if they intersected our world? Or if their shadows were cast into our world? Who knows? Maybe they'd look like simple shapes, such as squares, or maybe they'd look far more complicated. Maybe they'd look like buildings or cities or people.

Remember the man intersecting Flatland and looking to

the Flatlander like multiple separate objects (his legs, his fingers, his torso) even though he is actually just one object? The same would be true of a four–dimensional being intersecting our world. A single being might look to us like a bunch of separate buildings or people.

If the universe surrounding ours has more than four dimensions, things get even more complicated.

Hold that thought.

Upward Mobility

And now, finally, we get to the good stuff. I'm about to impart to you some secret and scary knowledge.

How do I know this scary secret stuff? you ask. Fair question.

In the novel *Flatland*, a sphere from the three-dimensional world tells the novel's two-dimensional protagonist about the existence of the three-dimensional world and what it's like. In exactly the same way, a being from the higher-dimensional world I'm going to tell you about whispered this secret knowledge into my ear.

I don't know his name. I don't even know if beings in his higher-dimensional universe have names as we understand them. I asked him what I should call him, but the question seemed to puzzle him. So I made up a name for him: Heidi, as in higher-dimensional dingus. (I don't think he found that amusing.) All of the shocking, stunning, horrifying secret knowledge that follows was either divulged to me by Heidi or deduced by me from what Heidi told me.

Or maybe I'm just making it all up.

I'm probably just making it all up.

For convenience, let's give a name to our familiar three-dimensional world. Let's call it OurSpace. This is where we live. It's the whole universe, according to all of our senses. It's all there is.

But it really isn't. Just as two-dimensional Flatland floats in OurSpace, so OurSpace floats in a higher-dimensional space, which I call CorpSpace, for a reason that will soon become apparent.

Is CorpSpace four-dimensional, having only one more dimension than our own? We have no way of knowing. Maybe it is four-dimensional. Maybe it's five-dimensional. Maybe it's 35-gazillion dimensional. We can't look out into it to see, just as a Flatlander can't look up into OurSpace. We can, however, detect its influence on OurSpace.

OurSpace teems with life. So does CorpSpace. As is true of life here, CorpSpace creatures are governed by the need to eat, to avoid being eaten, and to reproduce the rest of the time.

At the lower levels of CorpSpace life, these three needs are similar to what we observe in OurSpace, and they are satisfied in similar ways.

Well, basically similar. CorpSpace creatures are far more complex physically than OurSpace creatures because they are higher-dimensional. For example, sex involves not only many partners but also involves fitting together far more complex body parts in more than three dimensions. The entire process is much more complicated than it is for us. On the other hand, the results are incomparably more delightful. Unfortunately, bad sex in CorpSpace is really, really bad. In the same way, food is far more delicious than in OurSpace, and becoming food is far more awful.

But I digress.

Matters are quite different with other, higher CorpSpace life forms. For them, the three powerful urges are combined in one: the drive to absorb.

Let's start with the fact that in CorpSpace, everything eats everything else, or at least tries to. It's a nasty, violent place. Even the lowest-level predators sometimes kill and eat the highest beings in CorpSpace. That shouldn't surprise us. Look what happens to human bodies after death. They get eaten by the smallest, lowest-level beings in OurSpace. That can even happen to a live human who takes a nap in the wrong place.

When captured by a low-level predator, a CorpSpace being, high or low, is torn to pieces and digested, thus disappearing forever.

Moving up the food chain, the situation is more complicated. If the predator is a higher-level being, then, depending on the predator's needs, the prey might be broken up and integrated, its organs becoming new, subsidiary organs for the predator. In some cases, if the prey is also higher level, a rudimentary form of the prey's consciousness survives, supplementing the predator's own consciousness. In this way, the predator becomes larger and more powerful, both physically and mentally.

Remarkably, this even applies in rare cases to the lowest predatory creatures in CorpSpace. A simple, mindless being, little more than an eating machine, can acquire more complex organs and even rudimentary intelligence if it captures and eats the right prey.

This means that in CorpSpace, you can eat your way up the ladder. CorpSpace beings can literally move up the food chain. By adding their prey's organs and consciousness to their own, they become increasingly higher-level beings. It's as if an alligator that kills and eats human beings idiotic enough to swim in alligator-infested rivers not only satisfies its hunger but also gradually transforms into a human being! Now imagine that the alligator-become-human nonetheless retains its giant jaws, teeth, and taste for human flesh. That's pretty much the situation in CorpSpace. It's not a place you would choose to go on vacation, even if it were possible for you to get there.

We'll return to this, but first, let's talk about size, immense size, unimaginable size—although I am asking you to actually imagine it.

Our own universe, OurSpace, is stupendously big. The part of it that we can see with astronomical instruments is 93 billion light years in diameter. What's that in miles? you ask. It's 54 followed by 22 zeros miles. And that's just the part we can see. We don't know how big the whole thing actually is. There is presumably a whole lot of universe beyond what we can see.

Yes, that's very big. But it's minuscule compared to CorpSpace. CorpSpace is not only unimaginably bigger than OurSpace; it's also bigger in more ways. Remember that while OurSpace is big in height, width, and length, CorpSpace has more than three dimensions, so in addition to being mind-bogglingly bigger in height, width, and length than OurSpace, it's also mind-bogglingly bigger in...well, whatever the names for those other dimensions are.

The stupendous, unimaginable, inconceivable, etc. size of CorpSpace compared to OurSpace is a good thing. That's because of the intersections and projections we talked about earlier.

I said that CorpSpace teems with ravenously hungry life. Given how super-duper-gigantic CorpSpace is, that means there's an awful lot of life in it. Where does that life live? In the higher-dimensional equivalent of space? On the higher-dimensional equivalent of planetary surfaces? Inside stars? It's impossible to say. The physical structure of CorpSpace is beyond our ability to imagine. And it doesn't really matter, because all we're really interested in is how CorpSpace affects us.

As I said, it's fortunate for us that OurSpace occupies a tiny, tiny part of CorpSpace. Thanks to that tininess, most of the beings of CorpSpace are unaware of our existence. Not only is OurSpace so small from their perspective, it's also so flat, so boringly lacking in dimensions.

Here's an analogy. Think of a piece of thread. A tiny piece of thread lying on the ground is beneath our notice. That's how we look to CorpSpace beings. When you're walking around, even though you might not notice that piece of thread, it's possible that you'll step on it. You won't be aware that you've done so. You'll walk on uncaring. However, a tiny insect crawling along that piece of thread will have just experienced a catastrophe, probably a fatal one.

In exactly the same way, CorpSpace beings do occasionally blunder through our universe. They intersect it, to use the terminology I introduced earlier. Or they move between us and a source of higher-dimensional light in their universe, and they cast a shadow into OurSpace—a projection, as I called it before.

Those shadows appear, twist, change shape, and vanish as the CorpSpace being moves. We see them as something out of the corner of our eye that's no longer there when we look directly at the spot where they were. Or they may even look like human beings, but not quite—distorted shadows, ephemera, ghosts.

The unsettling feeling such almost–sightings give us is well described in the poem "Antigonish" by Hughes Mearns, who wrote it after hearing stories of a ghost that roamed a staircase in a house in Antigonish, Novia Scotia.

Antigonish

Yesterday, upon the stair,
I met a man who wasn't there
He wasn't there again today
I wish, I wish he'd go away...
When I came home last night at three
The man was waiting there for me
But when I looked around the hall
I couldn't see him there at all!
Go away, go away, don't you come back any more!
Go away, go away, and please don't slam the door...
(slam!)
Last night I saw upon the stair
A little man who wasn't there
He wasn't there again today
Oh, how I wish he'd go away...

Such sightings are unsettling, even frightening, but harmless.

Intersections are a different matter. Intersections, where a part of the CorpSpace being actually has form and shape in OurSpace, are very dangerous indeed.

CorpSpace dwellers are all vicious predators, remember. They are cruel as well. They kill for fun as well as sustenance and growth. CorpSpace has no equivalent of peaceniks, humanitarians, or gentle souls. Such beings do occasionally appear there due to an accident of higher–dimensional genetics, but they don't last long.

We have a lot of vicious predators of our own, of course, from microscopic ones that eat each other and in some cases also eat us, up to huge ones, such as Nile crocodiles, that will very happily swallow a human being in a very few gulps. But we know a lot about all of those. We've studied them extensively, both out of scientific curiosity and for purposes of self–defense.

CorpSpace beings' intersections with OurSpace are a different matter. We haven't studied them, we don't even know they exist, and we have no defense against them.

The intersections of lower–level CorpSpace creatures with OurSpace are just as hungry, vicious, and violent as the complete multidimensional creatures of which they are a part.

In our universe, they may appear as fantastical, nightmarish creatures: vampires, werewolves, ghouls, zombies, and so on—all the dreadful things that people have woven stories about for ages. Of course there's never any solid evidence for the existence of such creatures. That's because they only exist for as long as the CorpSpace creature intersects OurSpace. Remember the example of the man moving downwards through Flatland, taking on different appearances as he moved but finally dwindling to a point and then disappearing as he moved all the way through? In the same way, those CorpSpace intersections vanish entirely, leaving no trace, when the Corspace beings move entirely through OurSpace and then exit.

Fortunately, these intersections don't happen often. Again, that's because our entire universe is so tiny and negligible compared to CorpSpace. Those terrible predators aren't really aware of us. Their intersections with OurSpace are accidental, due mostly to their low-intelligence blundering about.

Whew.

At least that's the case with Earth. For all we know, the predators are aware of OurSpace and enjoy intersecting with it and hunting in it, but if so, then they're doing it far away from us. It could well be that there are whole planets with sentient races that live in constant terror and are regularly being torn to pieces in front of their friends and families, only to have the pieces themselves disappear from the universe as the predators carry them off into higher dimensions.

How awful! Well, it would be awful if this were happening here, to human beings. Fortunately, it's only happening, if it's happening at all, to weird-looking aliens on planets vast distances away from us. Let's not spend any more time thinking about them.

Because we have something to worry about right here on our own planet, and that is the very top of the CorpSpace food chain, where dwell the beings who are aware of us and who intersect our universe—our world!—deliberately, with dire consequences for us.

The Corpulence of Corps

We human beings are the top of the food chain here on Earth. We are the apex predator and the masters of nature. The apex predator of CorpSpace, master of all it surveys and inspiration for that universe's name, is a creature called a corp.

Of course they don't call themselves corps, just as Heidi doesn't call himself Heidi. Even if we could somehow hear their name for themselves, to us it would be a meaningless jumble of noise. I call them corps for a reason that will soon become apparent.

Corps are the biggest and best-fed beings in CorpSpace. Because of the manner in which the higher-level CorpSpace beings eat each other—the integration of the prey's organs, functions, and intelligence into the body and brain of the predator, as described earlier—corps are also far superior to all lower CorpSpace creatures in terms of physical and mental abilities.

As with everything else about CorpSpace beings, it's impossible for us to comprehend what those abilities are, what they mean, and how they function. Higher-dimensional existence is simply too different from our three-dimensional experience for any of it to make sense to us. Corps may be far more intelligent than anything in CorpSpace, but are they intelligent as we understand the word? Or are they simply stupendously large and frighteningly efficient multi-dimensional predators, like a super-duper version of a great white shark?

Based on their behavior, we can say that their intelligence is far more complex than that of a great white shark, and their appetite for absorbing and integrating lower-level beings, or even other corps, is limitless.

They're also quite sadistic. For example, one of their amusements is to attack a smaller, weaker corp, but instead of killing and absorbing it, they bite off a very large chunk and absorb that chunk, leaving their victim still alive, still functioning, but so weakened that it can never again be a competitor and lives in constant terror of the bigger corp that attacked it.

Even crueler, in a way, is the habit of some larger corps of attacking a smaller rival and, rather than biting anything off, instead penetrating the prey and removing and then absorbing some of its organs, leaving the smaller corp outwardly unchanged but dangerously downgraded, so crippled that it can easily be attacked and consumed by still smaller corps.

Why the great corps find any of this entertaining will probably always be beyond our ability to understand.

(If you do understand it, or even worse, if you like what you've just read, then I would prefer to have nothing to do with you. But I do hope you'll keep reading.)

The Ones That See Us

No doubt you're wondering what any of this has to do with us. The nature of CorpSpace sounds very unpleasant for all but the largest of the corps, and, even though I told you not to, you're probably feeling sorry for any alien civilizations unfortunate enough to experience frequent intersections with CorpSpace predators. But since those frequent intersections don't happen in our corner of OurSpace, what's the relevance to our lives?

Unfortunately, a few centuries ago as we measure time (time in CorpSpace is of course multidimensional, and therefore the measurement of it is incomprehensible to us), some higher-level corps did discover our existence. And by "our" I mean human beings living on the planet Earth.

Now, they could have intersected with our world in the same way that lower-level corps do, appearing to us as some sort of terrifying predator, and simply eaten us. But their strange ideas of amusement dictated a different course.

You see, it wasn't the existence of individual human beings that interested them. Instead, they were intrigued by our large organizations.

We have many types of large organizations on Earth, and there are a few different types of higher-level corps. As it happens, different types of corps are attracted to different earthly organizations, with different consequences for us, as I will detail.

If you like, you can think of what follows as a partial taxonomy of CorpSpace. It's very partial. Even if I could go to CorpSpace to collect specimens, I wouldn't.

Megacorps

Let's start with a particularly nasty type of corp that I'll call a megacorp.

The type of large human organization that attracted the attention of megacorps was what we call a corporation. Corporations resonated with megacorps. Corporations appeared to them as amusing little flattened, three–dimensional versions of themselves.

I've been talking about the intersections of CorpSpace beings with OurSpace as if they would always appear to be something like a human being. But the situation is actually far more complicated than that. The bigger corps, such as the megacorps, are so big and so multi–dimensional that their intersection with our universe is very complex and consists of many seemingly separate parts.

In fact, when a megacorp intersects with our universe, we see that intersection as one of our great corporations: a giant organization spread over many buildings, perhaps many countries, and filled with employees.

Harken back to the Flatlander who sees the intersection of Glittering Euphemisms, Inc. with Flatland and thinks it's a two–dimensional corporation, Flatland GE. In the same way, we look at the intersection of a megacorp with OurSpace and think we see a corporation, which is something very familiar to us. That's an illusion, but it looks real to us. It looks and behaves like a corporation, an organization of human beings and buildings and offices and factories and rulebooks. Oh, and money. Absurd amounts of money.

It's an illusion, but at the same time, it's not. It doesn't just seem real; it *is* real. Flatland GE behaves just like a Flatland corporation, so much so that there are Flatlanders working there who have no idea about the true nature of their employer. In the same way, the intersection of a megacorp with OurSpace really is a corporation. Ordinary human beings work there, oblivious, sharing office space with what seem to be fellow human beings but who are in fact nothing more than three-dimensional intersections with the internal organs of the parent megacorp.

That's why megacorps find our actual corporations so amusing and interesting.

In the Introduction, I talked about the odd way the nature of a company changes when it hits a certain size, usually somewhere between 50 and 100 employees. At that point, the company's feeling of familiarity changes to one of detachment and distance. Procedures and rules and handbooks appear. It's not as easy as it was before to take care of a problem by chatting with someone you know. Instead, you might have to have a meeting in a conference room with people you don't know at all. You pass many strangers in the hallways. The company has expanded from a small suite to a maze of offices on several floors, eventually to several buildings, and then to buildings in different cities or countries. The earnings numbers might look good, and perhaps so do the bonuses, but it no longer feels like a group of human beings working together.

The company itself, the corporation, is now the only being that counts. The humans come and go. They are interchangeable and disposable. The corporation persists.

You might think this is simply a case of emergent behavior—the whole is greater than the sum of its parts. When a company is young and small, you know or can fairly easily find out who founded it and when and where it was founded. If you work for such a small company, the founders and owners are probably working in the same office suite with you. If they're sensible, hard-working people, they might be sitting in a cubicle no bigger than yours.

But when the company hits that magical size, upper-level management is no longer nearby. It might be located on a higher floor in the same building, up in the rarefied atmosphere of the C-Suite. It might be in a different city. You can find documents filed with government agencies that supposedly provide you with details about the company, but they're dry and uninformative reading, and no one really checks those details unless wrongdoing is suspected.

If you work for a giant corporation, you might have experienced an in-person visit to your local office by a big shot from headquarters, someone dressed in an absurdly expensive suit, glossy, smarmy, and glad handing, and you might well have asked yourself, "Is this guy even human? Where do they find these people? Why was he put in charge of a major corporation?"

Years ago, when I worked for Glittering Euphemisms, an employee meeting was called so that we could enjoy the thrilling experience of watching the GE CEO, a guy I'll call Jehovah's Witness because that wasn't his name, be interviewed on television. JW was one of those CEOs who is often interviewed on TV and profiled in glossy business magazines. Such creatures are termed "thought leaders." They are portrayed as pioneers forging the path forward, leading America's corporatocracy ever higher and into ever brighter realms.

The interviewer asked questions, and JW babbled utter nonsense in response. His answers consisted of streams of English words, but they didn't add up to sentences. I whispered to a fellow employee that JW was spouting gibberish, only to be assured that JW was brilliant, that his mighty CEO brain was running far ahead of his mouth's ability to catch up, and it was evidence of the high level of his thought processes, far above the comprehension of us peasants.

(I retold this experience in fictional form in my satirical novel *Business Secrets from the Stars*, which you should read at the earliest opportunity and praise to friends, relatives, and passing strangers.)

Thanks to my higher-dimensional pal, I have come to understand what's really happening. It's not emergent behavior. Not at all. What is actually happening is much more sinister.

When an earthly corporation reaches a certain size—the 50 to 100 employee range that I mentioned—it becomes large enough to be noticed by a megacorp.

Sometimes, it is noticed only as possible prey. Despite being a paltry three-dimensional organization, it has developed interesting and tasty parts. And so, sometimes, a seemingly healthy corporation suddenly dwindles and ceases to exist, often with shocking suddenness. What really happened was that a megacorp noticed it and ate it.

What about the people, the actual OurSpace human beings, who worked there? Many, sensing trouble or looking for higher pay, leave in time (resign). Others are spat out (laid off) by the megacorp because they don't taste good or they don't serve the megacorp's needs. But some are absorbed, becoming part of the megacorp and continuing a minimal, semi-sentient existence somewhere out there in CorpSpace. You've surely worked with people you lost touch with, and then years later, when you wondered what had become of them and tried to track them down, you could find no trace of them. Now you know why. They were absorbed and transported out of our universe.

More often, a megacorp notices an OurSpace corporation, attacks it, and rips out only the tasty, interesting bits, leaving the rest to blunder on for a few months or years, blind and brainless, until it enters bankruptcy and vanishes. What of the people who worked in those tasty, interesting bits? Again, some leave in time, some are spat out, and others vanish from human ken.

But most often, the megacorp envelops and absorbs the earthly corporation and keeps it alive and operating as a part of the megacorp. The earthly corporation is now nothing more than the intersection of the megacorp with OurSpace. What was once a small company with a friendly, personal feeling is now exactly the cold, impersonal, alien creature it seems to be. The cumbersome rules, excessive procedures, and absurd corpspeak documents emanating from Human Resources really do come from an alien and irrational dimension. The same is true of the bizarre organization charts and the mentally twisted incompetents in upper management. They are all intersections, three-dimensional slices through their even more incomprehensible CorpSpace selves.

Fortunately, the now-alien corporation is still able to issue paychecks, and those checks don't bounce.

Until they do. Then the earthly corporation fades from existence (see above).

Dissecting the Intersections

If, during your working career, you have moved among large corporations, you will surely have noticed that certain types of employees repeat from one corporation to another. They are similar in personality and behavior, and often also in terms of their functions within the corporations.

Now, this is to be expected. It's a case of form following function, of similar people doing similar jobs. When you encountered those odd human duplicates, you probably told yourself that's all it was. But in some cases, these human repetitions resembled each other strikingly in appearance and sometimes even in mannerisms.

How strange, you thought. *Oh, I must be imagining things.*

You weren't.

Remember my example of a man intersecting Flatland and how his fingers would appear as separate but similar circular shapes? They looked similar but separate to the Flatlander, but in fact they weren't separate at all; they were part of the same three-dimensional human being. That's exactly what you were experiencing when you encountered those human duplicates. Instead of fingers sliced through by the plane that is Flatland, you were encountering the *same organ* of the megacorp intersecting our three-dimensional universe in different places and appearing as separate but similar organs here in OurSpace.

The intersection of a megacorp with OurSpace looks to us like a corporation. The megacorp's individual organs, when sliced through by OurSpace, appear to us as the organs that make up a corporation: buildings, chairs, desks, trucks, three-ring binders, and people.

Perhaps sometimes those human duplicates struck you as

shallow, pallid, lacking in depth. It's possible that those weren't even intersections but rather projections, shadows cast into OurSpace. I've known such "people" to disappear, and when I asked what had happened to so-and-so, the response was vague, evasive, and unsatisfactory. Probably something moved in CorpSpace, causing the shadow to vanish.

Oh, the Humanity

You will object that you know some of your coworkers in, let's say, Glittering Euphemisms. You have had drinks with them. You have met their spouses and children. These are clearly perfectly normal human beings. As are you yourself, of course.

Sure. Of course. Certainly there are actual human beings working for GE, great numbers of them, just as there are great numbers of actual Flatlanders working for Flatland GE. But how many of your tens of thousands of fellow GE workers do you know personally? You have encountered only a tiny fraction of the whole, and even then you didn't deal with most of them in person, but rather via emails, phone calls, and video conferences. You've had drinks or meals with an even tinier fraction of the whole, and you've met the spouses and children of a fraction of that tiny fraction.

Moreover, you don't have to work for a great corporation for very long to learn that the higher up the corporate ladder employees are, the less human they seem to be. You have very probably had the experience of watching a formerly friendly coworker be promoted and quickly become far less friendly—and, well, less human.

Isn't this simply due to the corporate class system, the social structure that dictates that as one moves up the ladder, one must look only sideways and upwards for social contacts? No doubt that's so in many cases. Sleazy behavior has been with us for longer than we have been human beings, and alien intervention from higher dimensions isn't required to explain it. But think about those formerly friendly coworkers, now above you on the corporate ladder, who are now cold and distant. Do you really think that social-class snobbishness explains all of the change in them? Aren't there some such people whose personality changes are unprecedented, even inexplicable?

What happened in those cases is that they were absorbed by the megacorp. The outer shell remained. They looked unchanged, but the prey had become merely an organ of the megacorp, living a shadowy semblance of life, outwardly a sentient being, inwardly hollow and empty.

On the bright side, their upward path through the corporate hierarchy is now assured.

In addition to those people, aren't there coworkers who were cold and unapproachable from the moment you met them? Some of them were probably just shy, but only some of them. The others were not human at all. They were nothing more than intersections, three-dimensional slices through megacorp internal organs. I hope you didn't eat anything they touched in the break room.

Corps feed on smaller corps, as mentioned earlier. Some of them also feed on humans. That can be literal feeding, which explains many cases of human employees disappearing, or it can be a kind of life-energy vampirism.

New human employees are typically full of youthful

enthusiasm and energy. That's how *we* describe them. However, the vampiric megacorp would describe them as "juicy." Not for long, though. As the years pass, the human employee, if lucky enough to be allowed to remain human, shrinks and shrivels, fades, and soon seems sucked dry. You've surely noticed that in long-time employees. You might be afraid that it's happening to you. You're not imagining things.

Eventually, sucked dry, the employee is discarded by the corporation and replaced with another human, a younger—juicier!—one.

But what about the grotesquely overpaid, babbling fools one finds at the top levels in so many giant corporations? Wouldn't the earthly goals of a corporation be better served by filling those positions with competent, intelligent, real human beings?

You would think so, but that's because you're making the mistake of thinking that those goals really are the ones touted in corpspeak-filled corporate PR nonsense. In fact, once a corporation is absorbed by a megacorp, it exists only to amuse the megacorp, that vicious, sadistic predator, which derives the most amusement from sucking its human employees dry and wreaking destruction as widely as possible.

Once you understand that, you will understand corporatocracy and capitalism.

Policorps

When a political party reaches a certain size and influence, it can attract the attention of a certain type of corp, which then absorbs the party, so that the party becomes the corp's intersection with OurSpace in the same way earthly corporations are absorbed by megacorps. That process explains why a political party can change from espousing fairly sane policies to spewing evil and nonsensical ones.

Consider how quickly exactly that happened to the Republican Party in the United States.

The type of corp doing this type of predation we will call a policorp. It is fascinated by our political parties and by human politics in general, in all its many forms across the Earth.

Policorps may be fascinated by our politics, but they can't make heads or tails of it. However, that doesn't matter. Remember that all varieties of corps are predators driven to eat and grow. They are also so constituted as to derive the greatest pleasure from eating when they can inflict great pain in the process. The greater the pain, the greater their pleasure. For that reason, policorps don't have to understand OurSpace politics to be attracted to it and delighted by its power to do harm.

We may talk of politics inflicting damage, but it's really political parties doing the inflicting, and it's those parties that policorps are drawn to. Of course they're aware of the ability of political parties to do great good—for example, Franklin Delano Roosevelt and his New Deal—but it's the power to harm that attracts the policorps. To them, human politics is vastly entertaining and attractive because the evil potential in political parties is delightful.

Even a political party that is too small to have much power or influence can attract a policorp if the party's evil is sufficiently intense. To the higher-dimensional senses of a policorp, intense political evil is a beacon shining out of our three-dimensional universe into higher-dimensional space. Hitler's Nazi Party is a fine example. Long before it attained power, when it was still seen as a joke by most Germans, its terrible potential was clear and it became an extension of a particularly nasty and evil policorp.

But we don't have to look for quite such a degree of evil to detect the process of absorption. Nor does the potential to destroy society have to be that extreme to attract the attention of a policorp. America's own Republican Party was consumed by a particularly nasty policorp at roughly the time Richard Nixon became the party's presidential nominee in 1960. That policorp was still learning the ways of American politics. In addition, it was distracted by events in CorpSpace and took its eye off the ball. As a result, the Republican Party—the three-dimensional manifestation of a policorp of unusual vileness—lost the election that year and then again four years later. But instead of giving up and withdrawing from OurSpace, the policorp kept learning and growing new organs of nastiness.

The electoral results have been hit or miss, a combination of victories and defeats. But all along, the party has been spreading its evil influence throughout American society, befogging minds and corrupting souls. The policorp is very happy.

The distinction between corp subspecies seems to be even fuzzier than that between animal species in our world. There is, for example, quite an overlap between policorps and megacorps. That overlap shows up in OurSpace in the form of unholy marriages between corporations and political parties. German businesses were in bed with the Nazis from an early date, and in our own time we see the same deadly copulation.

In particular, in America, in 2024, we experienced a presidential election, the outcome of which was so horrifying, so irrational, so self-destructive, that it can only be explained as the result of manipulation by a monstrously evil being from beyond time and space.

As I said, megacorps also intersect with our politics. Usually, they operate behind the scenes—by donating money to political parties, for example, or, as happened in America's 2024 election, by manipulating consumer prices so as to persuade the gullible masses to vote against a political party dominated by actual human beings and instead to vote for one whose leadership consists of creatures who may appear human but who are in fact intersections—soulless, three-dimensional manifestations of CorpSpace evil.

In some cases, as we are seeing now, meddlesome megacorps amuse themselves by having their CEO appendage-intersections show public support for the ghastly politician appendage-intersection through whom they intend to wreak destruction in our world.

Indeed, the creature who has been placed on the pinnacle of power by the 2024 election—a rough approximation of a human being that I'll refer to as Gibbon, both because he makes me think of that primate flinging feces and because he reminds me of loony incompetents presiding over the destruction of a great empire—is clearly the intersection of OurSpace with a diseased organ of a megacorp that has merged with the policorp that absorbed the Republican Party. I suppose we should call the result if the merger a megapolicorp.

To help further the illusion that Gibbon is human, the megapolicorp has intersected some of its other body parts with OurSpace to provide him/it with a succession of "wives." I assume that the megapolicorp is still learning the ways of OurSpace, and that's why it has been unable to avoid having the "wife" intersections look so much alike.

Come to think of it, this flaw extends to almost all of the highly visible Republican "wives." Perhaps the megapolicorp will improve with practice.

I've said that the nature of corps is to be predatory, and that includes cannibalism. Surprisingly, we are witnessing a kind of chumminess between some of the OurSpace intersections of different corps. In particular, highly visible intersections of three different megacorps, human simulacra that I'll call Loon, Zebos, and Suck, have been outspoken in their support of Gibbon.

From a purely mundane perspective, this would make sense if all four of these intersections actually were human beings and CorpSpace didn't exist. Gibbon's time in power will benefit their three earthly corporations tremendously, in addition to his own. In reality, though, CorpSpace does exist, and the megacorps that are manipulating those seeming human beings like meat puppets are salivating at the thought of the destruction and agony they will soon be visiting upon our world.

I will admit to some surprise at how poor a job the four corps have done with those particular intersections. Gibbon, Loon, Zebos, and Suck don't act or sound all that human, do they? In particular, Gibbon has been malfunctioning severely lately. It will probably soon be absorbed back into the parent megapolicorp, possibly to be replaced with an even more repulsive pseudo–human. Perhaps when they created those intersections, the four corps were so fixated on doing evil that they got sloppy.

I haven't even mentioned Gibbon's odious little sidekick, Glance, partly because he seems scarcely worth mentioning, and partly because he's been invisible recently. He's obviously not human, but it's not clear exactly what he is. A projection, a mere shadow? A partial intersection, too incomplete to appear convincingly human? And where is he? Perhaps one of the rival megacorps or policorps ate him. No one seems to have noticed.

Mind you, this chumminess won't last. The corps' true nature will reassert itself, and they will attack each other, tearing off chunks and absorbing them, gouging out organs, and so on. Perhaps that won't happen until they've sated themselves with death and destruction. Let's hope it won't take that long. In any case, at some point, they will turn on each other and revert to their proper nature. What will that look like from our earthly perspective? I don't know, but those of us who are still alive at that point will probably find the results entertaining.

Theocorps

Another type of corp that has noticed us, resulting in great damage to our world, is one I'll call a theocorp.

These creatures are irrational and dangerous even by CorpSpace standards. They are attracted to what we call organized religions, but unlike other corps, they show interest even when a religious organization is small and young and just starting to destroy minds—a cult, that is to say. Even a cult is destructive enough to tickle the fancy of a theocorp, although theocorps do prefer much larger religious organizations because their capacity for harm is so great.

I mentioned their extreme irrationality. They are especially charmed by the nonsensical babbling of clerics. It mirrors the nonsense that passes for a theocorp's internal dialogue. Thus, when a theocorp absorbs an earthly religion and replaces its clerics with parts of itself, the flow of absurdities continues uninterrupted with no differences noticed by the religion's human adherents.

A major aspect of their deep irrationality is the theocorps' hatred of science. It is their collective mission to destroy it and all logical thought along with it. Human history shows how successful they have been.

Like the crows of our world, theocorps are fascinated by

shiny things. When a theocorp intersects with OurSpace, merging with an earthly religious organization, that fascination manifests itself as an affinity for an excess of gaudy, tasteless decorations. And, of course, money. Lots and lots of money, the possession of astonishing amounts of which can be seen in the mansions, cars, and private jets flaunted by many of the human-shaped parts of the intersections.

A very large percentage of those human-shaped intersections, which we call the clergy, are also drawn to sex of the sorts condemned by their religious organizations. I suspect that the parent theocorps are amused by this hypocrisy.

I mentioned the increasing cooperation between megacorps and policorps, at least in terms of their intersections with OurSpace. To make matters more complicated, theocorps have been getting into the game as well. That's true especially in America, where it's almost as if some sort of three-way merger is taking place. Perhaps we're just seeing three-dimensional echoes of a feeding frenzy that's happening in CorpSpace. Whatever the underlying cause, down here in our world, we are witnessing the emergence of the megapolitheocorp, a creature as dangerous to civilization as its name is cumbersome.

The Arts

Articorps believe they are the most powerful, influential, and important of all the corps. In fact, the opposite is the case. They are so insignificant that not even the smallest and weakest of corps bother to eat them. Some of the lowest-level and most simpleminded of the creatures of CorpSpace might occasionally try a nibble, but even they normally pass on other prey, finding the articorps to be too lacking in nourishment to bother.

Still, driven by their hugely exaggerated sense of their own importance, many articorps have joined the game of intersecting with OurSpace and absorbing, and thus replacing, native organizations. As I'm sure you've guessed from the name I gave them, their OurSpace prey consists of arts organizations.

Once absorbed by an articorp, the earthly intersection mimics the behavior of its parent creature. It touts the immense and fundamental importance of its own particular art form. Generally speaking, it encounters much the same reaction from ordinary humans as the parent articorp does from other corps. That is, it is ignored.

Not entirely, of course. Human beings love to be entertained. Perhaps it's more accurate to say that we love to escape from our daily reality, and the arts have always provided such an escape. To the extent that the arts do this, they are loved by humans.

That's not enough for the articorp extensions, however. Their claim to great importance ignored, they turn inward. They become intellectually incestuous and creatively vacuous. They devote a good deal of their time to developing obscure, arcane, nonsensical versions of their art forms and trying to bully human beings into liking those. Then, when they fail, they complain bitterly and sneeringly.

But that's enough about articorps, and probably more than they deserve.

Parenting

Bear with me while I speculate, going beyond the limits of the knowledge imparted to me by Heidi.

It's an odd fact of life that parents are so similar across cultures. It's as if there were only a few actual parents, and those repeat over time and space. Even stranger is the common observation that as time passes, and entirely against our will, we turn into our parents.

It's probably just a quirk of human nature—genetics combined with the stresses of daily life and hormones and who knows what else.

Or just possibly there is a type of corp, call it an ohmomcorp, whose intersections with OurSpace somehow partially absorb human parents. Perhaps there are only a few ohmomcorps that have discovered OurSpace, and perhaps a typical ohmomcorp has vast numbers of tendrils that each intersects OurSpace. A single ohmomcorp would then appear to be millions of parents all over the world and throughout time, all of them disturbingly like each other.

This would certainly explain a lot and would account for much of the misery in the world. On the other hand, it does seem very far-fetched, doesn't it? So I'm probably just getting carried away and seeing the influence of corps everywhere, even in cases where the blame for our unhealthy ways lies squarely on our own shoulders.

But it would explain much that we've all observed, doesn't it?

No, no. Surely not.

And yet...

No.

Milcorps

National militaries are the largest and most destructive organizations of all. Surely there are corps particularly attracted to them—milcorps, let's call them.

Heidi said nothing about them when he was telling me about the various types of corps and what interests them in OurSpace, so I asked him whether milcorps existed in CorpSpace, and if so, what they were like. He didn't answer me. When I pressed him on the matter, he became evasive. When I persisted, he grew hostile, so I stopped.

I think he was frightened.

Thus, on the question of milcorps, your guess is good as mine and possibly as disturbing.

But I wonder. Will we ever see the emergence of a megapolitheomilcorp? I fear that would herald the end of our civilization.

Meanwhile, Down Here

Are there even higher-dimensional spaces meddling in CorpSpace the way CorpSpace meddles in OurSpace? And still higher-dimensional spaces above those meddling in them? And so on, ever upward? I have no idea, and when I asked my CorpSpace contact those very questions, he got huffy. As you have probably gathered by now, it's not a good idea to annoy a corp. Therefore, I desisted.

But is he a corp? He never said so! Why did he choose to impart this secret knowledge to me? Is he part of a power struggle in CorpSpace? Is he from somewhere else, perhaps some other dimension entirely, meddling in both CorpSpace and OurSpace for inscrutable alien reasons of his own? It makes me uneasy to ponder those questions.

I suppose those questions are of no real importance to us, though. Our concern is down here, in our boring, flat, dull, three-dimensional existence. Down here where we now know that all is not as it seems, that awful forces are at play behind the seemingly placid exterior we see, that so many of those we thought were our fellow human beings are in fact aspects of terrifying predatory creatures from a higher dimension.

How dreadful! This little book certainly paints a depressing view of things, doesn't it?

Fortunately, it's a mere flight of fancy.

About the Author

David Dvorkin was born in 1943 in Reading, England. His family moved to South Africa after World War II, and then to the United States when David was a teenager. After attending college in Indiana, he worked at NASA in Houston on the Apollo Project, then at Martin Marietta in Denver on the Viking Mars lander project. His aerospace career ended in 1974. Thereafter, until 2009, he worked as a software developer and technical writer. He and his wife, Leonore, and their son, Daniel, have lived in Denver since 1971.

In addition to non-fiction, David has published many science fiction, horror, and mystery novels. For details, as well as quite a bit of nonfiction reading material, please see David's website: http://www.dvorkin.com/

Social Media

Facebook: http://www.facebook.com/DavidDvorkin
Bluesky: @nikrovd.bsky.social
Twitter: http://twitter.com/David_Dvorkin
Blog: http://eyeblister.blogspot.com/

www.ingramcontent.com/pod-product-compliance
Lightning Source LLC
Chambersburg PA
CBHW070623310726
48982CB00001B/160
* 9 7 8 1 7 3 6 2 8 8 6 7 2 *